Gemma
the Gymnastics
Fairy

For Gemma Poole,
with lots of love

Special thanks to
Sue Mongredien

ISBN 978-0-545-20258-9

18   16/0

Printed in the U.S.A.   40

First Scholastic Printing, April 2010

Gemma
the
Gymnastics
Fairy

by Daisy Meadows

SCHOLASTIC INC.

New York   Toronto   London   Auckland
Sydney   Mexico City   New Delhi   Hong Kong

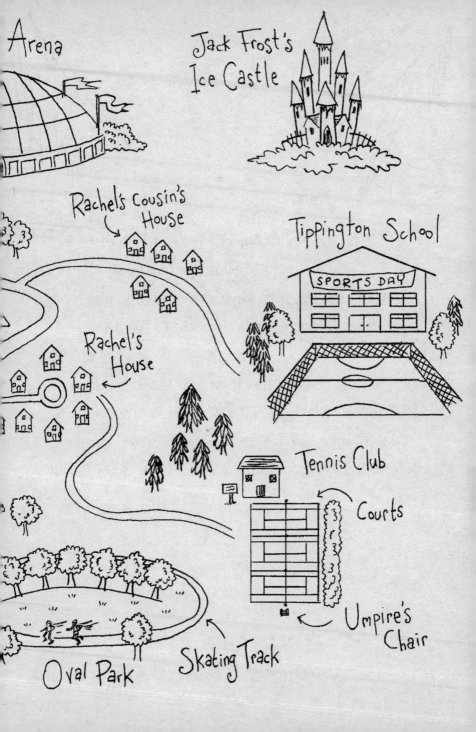

Arena

Jack Frost's
Ice Castle

Rachel's Cousin's
House

Tippington School

SPORTS DAY

Rachel's
House

Tennis Club

Courts

Umpire's
Chair

Oval Park

Skating Track

The Fairyland Olympics are about to start,
And my crafty goblins will take part.
We'll win this year, for I have a cunning plan.
I'll send my goblins to compete in Fairyland.

The magic objects that make sports safe and fun
Will be stolen by my goblins, to keep until we've won.
Sports Fairies, prepare to lose and to watch us win.
Goblins, follow my commands, and let the games begin!

Contents

Someone in School

"Almost there," Rachel Walker said as she and her best friend, Kirsty Tate, walked along a sunny street. "Aunt Joan lives around the corner, near my school."

"That's good," Kirsty said, glancing down at the basket they were carrying. "These chocolate Easter eggs might melt if we had to go any farther!"

Kirsty was staying with Rachel's family for spring vacation, and the two girls were delivering Easter presents to Rachel's cousins.

"I can't believe it's Friday already," Rachel said. "The Fairyland Olympics start today!"

Kirsty nodded. "And we still haven't found Gemma the Gymnastics Fairy's magic hoop," she said. "If we don't get it back from the goblins soon, then all the gymnastics events at the Olympics will be ruined. It would be horrible!"

The girls were having a very exciting week, helping the Sports Fairies find their missing magic objects. The magic objects ensured that sports were fun and safe for everyone in the human world, as well as in Fairyland. But the magic objects worked only when they were with their rightful owners, the Sports Fairies.

Jack Frost knew the magic objects were so powerful that they made anyone who was holding them—and even someone who was simply close to them—very talented at that particular sport. He had sent his goblins to steal the sports objects so that they could use them to cheat in the Olympic Games. Jack Frost wanted his goblins to be the winning team. He knew that the winners would receive a golden cup full of luck as the grand prize—and he really wanted it for himself.

The goblins had taken the magic objects into the human world to use while they practiced their sports. Because the magic objects weren't where they were supposed to be, sports in Fairyland and the human world had been going horribly! There had been all kinds of confusion and clumsiness.

The girls passed Tippington School, and Kirsty suddenly stopped. "That's strange," she said, staring across the playground. "I just saw some kids inside the school, dressed in green."

"School's closed for vacation," Rachel told her. "And our uniforms are blue and gray, not green."

The same thought came to both girls at the same time, and they let out a gasp. "Goblins!" cried Rachel.

"If they *are* goblins, they might have Gemma's magic hoop with them," Kirsty said excitedly.

They gazed at the school, but there was no sign of anyone in there now. "Let's quickly drop off these Easter eggs, then look around a little more," Rachel suggested.

She and Kirsty rushed to Rachel's aunt's house. They knocked on the door, but there was no answer. They set the

basket down on the porch, out of the sun.

They hurried back to the school, but the main doors were locked. "Let's try around the back," Rachel said, leading the way. Then she and Kirsty froze as they heard the sound of someone whistling.

They peeked around the wall to see a man with his back to them, painting some bookcases. "It's our janitor," Rachel whispered. "Look, he left the door open. Let's sneak in."

Hearts pounding, the girls tiptoed in through the open door.

"It's very quiet," Kirsty commented. "Maybe I imagined it."

"Well, let's check out the gym while we're here," Rachel said. "Follow me."

Rachel led Kirsty down a long hallway until they reached a door. "This is where the gym equipment is stored," she said. "We can go through here into the gym itself."

She opened the door and a volleyball rolled out. Frowning,

Rachel picked it up and went inside. "What a mess!" she said with surprise. "It's not usually like this."

Kirsty followed. A pile of gym mats had been knocked over, there were balls scattered everywhere, and some goal posts lay on the floor. Her heart thumped with excitement. People inside the school, a mess in the gym closet . . . something strange was definitely going on!

The girls approached the other door, opened it a crack, and peeked out. Kirsty held back a gasp. She couldn't believe her eyes. The gymnasium was a blur of green. There were goblins everywhere!

Training Time

The two girls stared in silence. There were goblins swinging from the horizontal bar and from rings that dangled from the ceiling. Other goblins were leaping over the vault, dancing along the balance beam, and tumbling across the floor mats.

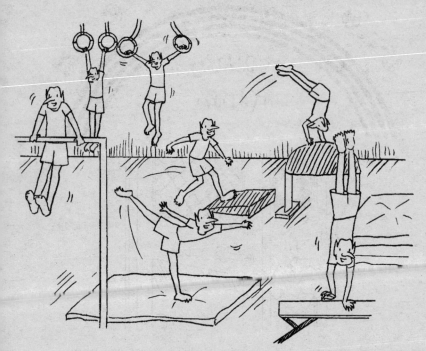

"Wow," Kirsty said, unable to drag
her eyes away, "They're fantastic!
The magic hoop must be close by for
all of the goblins to be performing so
well!"

Rachel nodded. Then a flash of blue
caught her eye, and she nudged Kirsty.
"Look!" she whispered, pointing.

Kirsty turned, and saw a goblin easily twirling a bright blue hoop around one arm. The hoop shimmered with blue sparkles. "That definitely looks like fairy magic," she breathed with excitement.

The goblin sent the hoop rolling across one of the gym mats, while he performed a series of perfect handsprings alongside it. Then he landed on his feet, grabbed the hoop, and bowed deeply to an imaginary audience.

"That must be Gemma's hoop," Rachel whispered. "The last magic sports object!"

"There's something else sparkling in

here, too," Kirsty said, suddenly noticing a tiny flash of light in a dark corner.

Rachel turned to see Gemma the Gymnastics Fairy come spiraling up out of a pile of hoops, in a burst of yellow sparkles.

Gemma wore a pale blue leotard and yellow leggings. Her hair was twisted up in a bun, and her wings were tipped with gold.

"Hello, Gemma!" Kirsty said in delight. "Perfect timing—we think we've spotted your hoop."

Gemma beamed. "Hooray!" she said. "I just came from Fairyland, where all the athletes are busy with their last-minute practice sessions. The opening ceremony for the Olympics will be starting soon. We just have to get my hoop back in time!"

"Yes, the goblins are practicing too," Kirsty remarked.

But Rachel was lost in thought. Gemma's and Kirsty's words had given her an idea. "That's it!" she cried. "We could help the goblins practice!"

Kirsty stared at her, wondering if she'd heard correctly. "*Help* the goblins?"she repeated in surprise.

Rachel grinned. "If we offer to train the goblins, we'll have a good chance of getting close to Gemma's hoop," she explained.

Gemma cartwheeled through the air.

"Yes!" she cried. "And we might even teach them that you can get better at a sport without having to cheat. You just need to practice!" She smiled. "Now, let's see . . . I know how I can help." She waved her wand at the girls, and golden fairy dust whirled around them. In the twinkling of an eye, their clothes changed.

Rachel and Kirsty looked at each other
and smiled. They were now wearing
matching warm-up suits and gym shoes,
with stopwatches on their wrists. Their
hair had been pulled up into ponytails,
and there were silver whistles around their

necks. Baseball
caps helped hide
the girls' faces, so
that the goblins
wouldn't easily
see through their
disguise. "Look
at our T-shirts!"
Kirsty giggled,
pointing. Rachel

looked down and saw that K & R GOBLIN
TRAINING TEAM was written in glittery
silver letters on her shirt.

Gemma flew up to perch on Kirsty's ponytail, where her wings made her look kind of like a shiny hair bow. "Now to start training those goblins," she said. "And get the magic hoop!"

"Let's go," Kirsty agreed. She and Rachel pushed open the doors and walked into the gym, blowing their whistles loudly.

The goblins all stopped in surprise. One goblin was so startled, he lost concentration during his floor routine and tumbled head over heels onto the mat. He picked himself up and scooted over to another goblin. "Who are they?" the girls heard him whisper.

"Listen up, goblins!" shouted Kirsty. "This is your last chance to get in shape before the Fairyland Olympics! And we're going to help you, so line up in front of me! Move it! Move it!"

Rachel held her breath. For their plan to work, the goblins had to let her and Kirsty help with their training. But none of the goblins had moved a muscle to line up. Was the plan doomed before it had even started?

Gymnastic Fantastic

"Come on!" Rachel cried, clapping her hands. "You don't want those fairies to beat you in the Olympics, do you? We're here to make you gymnastic fantastic, so you have a chance of winning gold medals!"

"I want a medal!" one goblin called out from the crowd, running to start a line in front of Kirsty.

"Me, too!" cried another.

"And me, and me!" called some of the other goblins, as they rushed to get in line.

The one with the magic hoop was in the middle and demanded that the others give him more room. "Look at me!" he cried, swiveling the hoop around his hips at lightning speed.

"We want you all to practice your back handsprings first," Rachel said. "You can demonstrate," she added, pointing at the goblin with the magic hoop.

She held her breath as the goblin walked to the edge of the mat. She had noticed the way he'd let go of the hoop when he'd practiced his back handsprings earlier. If he did the same thing again, she might be able to grab it!

As Rachel had hoped, the goblin sent the magic hoop rolling before flipping along next to it. Unfortunately, the hoop spun by so fast, it was impossible for Rachel and Kirsty to even think about running to catch

it. And as soon as the goblin had finished, he grabbed it again.

Kirsty and Rachel exchanged glances. They'd have to try again later.

"OK, who's next?" Rachel asked.

"Me! Me! ME!" shouted the goblins, trying to push one another out of the way.

Kirsty blew her whistle. "It's your turn," she decided, pointing to a goblin with big ears. "Show us what you've got!"

One by one, the goblins took turns performing back handsprings across the floor. They weren't quite as good as the goblin with the magic hoop, but they all tried hard.

Meanwhile, the goblin with the magic
hoop was showing off to a group of
goblins in a corner of the gym. "Watch
this!" he yelled, breaking into a run
across the gym floor. He ran to the vault
and bounded over it, tossing the hoop
high into the air as he did so. He turned
a perfect somersault and then landed

feet–first through the falling hoop.

Everyone burst into applause, including Kirsty, Rachel, and Gemma.

"He won't be able to do that in the Olympic contest," Rachel heard one goblin mutter to another. "Jack Frost is going to shrink the hoop really small so the judges won't even know he has it. Clever, huh?"

Gemma flinched. "I can't stand cheating," she whispered to Kirsty. "It makes me so angry!"

But watching the performance had given Kirsty an idea. "Let's make an obstacle course for the goblins," she suggested. "You saw how the goblin had to throw the magic hoop when he vaulted. Well, there are other gymnastics moves where he'd have to let it go, too."

Rachel's eyes grew wide. "Yes," she said, "and we could even end the course with a ring toss—where the goblins

have to throw a hoop over me or you.
Then the goblin with the magic hoop
will have to throw it right to us!"

"Oh, that's perfect!" cried Gemma, in
her silvery voice. "Let's do it!"

Overcoming Obstacles

Kirsty blew her whistle again. "You did a great job on your back handsprings," she told the goblins. "Now we're going to set up an obstacle course for you. Please practice your forward and backward somersaults while we do that."

The goblins immediately began rolling around on the floor, pausing every so often to argue with one another.

Meanwhile, Kirsty and Rachel quickly arranged some pieces of equipment to make an obstacle course. Then Rachel clapped her hands to get the goblins' attention.

"This is what you need to do," she said. "Start by walking on your hands along the balance beam. Then run over to the horizontal bar and do three flips on it."

"Next," Kirsty said, "you turn upside down on the rings, vault over the horse, and tumble across the mat while twirling a ribbon."

"Finally," Rachel explained, "each of you has to toss a hoop over Kirsty,

who'll be standing at the other end of
the gym." She held up her stopwatch.
"I'll time you all. I wonder who'll be the
fastest?"

"I'll be the fastest," a tall goblin
boasted. "Just you wait!"

"No way!" the goblin with big ears
argued. "I'll be faster than you."

Kirsty pointed to a small goblin at
the front. "You can go first," she said
encouragingly.
"Ready, set, go!"

Rachel started
her stopwatch as
the small goblin set
off. He flipped into
a handstand and
carefully walked
along the balance

beam. His legs wobbled slightly, but
he managed not to fall. Then he ran
to the horizontal bar and performed

three flips—but he
was enjoying himself
so much that he kept
doing more and more!
"Wheeee!" he squealed,
tumbling around.

"OK, onto the rings now," Rachel
reminded him.

The goblin swung upside-down on
the rings and vaulted over the horse.
Then he grabbed a ribbon and began
a series of cartwheels and handsprings
across the mat, spiraling the ribbon as he
went. Unfortunately, he lost his balance
several times, and dropped his ribbon
once on the last section.

"Don't worry," Rachel said. "We can work on that later. Now grab a hoop from the pile, stand behind the line, and take your best shot."

The goblin took a hoop, steadied himself, and then threw it toward Kirsty. The hoop bounced off Kirsty's arm and clattered to the floor.

"Good try," Kirsty called.

"Your time was three minutes, thirty seconds," Rachel told him. "Next!"

It took a while for all the goblins to go through the course. The goblin with the magic hoop insisted on going last. "What's

the fastest time so far?" he asked as he stood at the starting line.

"Two minutes, forty seconds," Rachel replied.

The goblin looked scornful. "I'll beat that easily!" he declared.

"Ready, set, go!" Rachel called, blowing her whistle.

Off went the goblin, mounting the beam with a spectacular leap. He tossed the hoop into the air as he went into a handstand and caught it on one foot, balancing it perfectly as he moved along the beam.

"Wow!" Kirsty muttered under her breath to Gemma. "That's impressive."

At the end of the beam, the goblin
dismounted with a double backflip,
sending the hoop
flying into the air.
As he landed, he
caught it neatly
and then ran on
to the horizontal

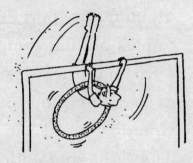

bar. With the hoop looped over one
shoulder, he did three perfect flips at a
dizzying speed.

It was quite a show. The goblin sped
through the rest of the obstacle course
without a single mistake. The other
goblins watched open-mouthed, too
amazed to even argue with one another.

He was making record time when
he came to the last part of the
challenge—the ring toss. He looked

suspiciously at Kirsty and held on tight to the magic hoop. "Hoop-tossing is not a gymnastic sport," he said. "I'm going to pass on that stunt."

Kirsty bit her lip. She had to think of something fast, otherwise their plan wouldn't work! She shrugged. "Oh, dear," she said with sympathy. "Are you worried you won't be as good as the others?"

"No way!" the goblin snapped.
"Watch this!" And he tossed the hoop
high into the air.

The girls and Gemma held their
breath as it rose into the air and spun
above Kirsty's head. . . .

Frost in Fairyland

The hoop landed perfectly over Kirsty's head, and the goblins all burst into a round of applause.

The goblin who'd thrown it smirked and bowed. Then he walked toward Kirsty, obviously wanting to take the hoop back.

But Kirsty was too quick for him.

She stepped out of the hoop, picked it
up, and held it in the air for Gemma.
The fairy flew down to it immediately.
As soon as Gemma's fingers closed
around it, the hoop magically shrank
down to its Fairyland size. Then Gemma
touched it with her wand, and there was
a flash of golden sparkles. The hoop's
magic was working properly again!

"Hey!" cried one of the goblins.
"It's one of those meddling fairies—and
she's got our hoop!"

"Someone get it back!" yelled another
goblin. "Otherwise we'll never win
anything at the Olympics!"

The goblins all made a mad dash for
the girls and Gemma, knocking into one
another in their
rush to get the
hoop. Kirsty
and Rachel
looked at
each other
in alarm
as the mob
of angry
goblins rushed
toward them,

but Gemma waved her wand and
turned the girls into
fairies—just in time!
Rachel's heart thumped
as she fluttered out of
the goblins' reach.
That was close!

Gemma waved her
wand again, and all
the pieces of
gym equipment
sparkled with
thousands of tiny
golden lights before
dancing back into
their appropriate
places in the gym closet.
The goblins watched in
bewilderment, their eyes wide.

As the last hoop rolled away, Gemma grinned at them. "See you in Fairyland," she said. "Don't be late—or you'll miss the opening ceremony of the Olympics!" Before any of the goblins could reply, Gemma had waved her wand a third time, and she and the girls were swept up in a magical whirlwind. "Off we go to Fairyland!" Kirsty and Rachel heard her call in a merry tune.

A few seconds later, the girls felt themselves float downward, and the whirlwind cleared.

"We're in the Fairyland Arena again!" Kirsty declared.

Rachel whistled. "And look how full it is."

The girls had been in the arena
once already, on the first day of
this adventure. But then it had been
completely empty. Now the seats were
filled with excited fairies, elves, pixies,
and goblins, all chatting about the
Olympics.

Kirsty could have happily spent
days gazing around at the sights. A
tall, green frog was selling official
programs in one row. A group of pixie
cheerleaders danced in the center of the
arena. And the fans all waved colorful
flags and banners to show which
contestants they were supporting. Some
of the flags were magical and kept
changing color. Some even seemed to
be playing music!

They had landed near the side of the arena, but Gemma led them straight to the center, where the fairy king and queen greeted them warmly. Then the king handed Gemma a sparkly gold microphone, so that she could speak to the crowd.

"Hello, everyone," Gemma said, waving. "I'm pleased to announce that

Kirsty and Rachel have helped us get all the magic sports objects back, including my magic hoop!"

A huge cheer rose from the crowd, but not from the goblin section. They looked obviously frustrated by the news. But the fairies, pixies, elves, and other magical people were all clapping, cheering, and waving their flags with joy.

GOBLINZ To WIN!

The king and queen looked delighted, too. "Thank you," King Oberon said to Kirsty and Rachel. "You have helped save our Olympic Games! Without you, the goblins would have had an unfair advantage."

"Now that the magic objects are back with our Sports Fairies, the games will be a fair contest." Queen Titania smiled. "We are very grateful."

Kirsty and Rachel curtsied, feeling very proud. But then the air turned cold.

Rachel shivered and rubbed her arms. "Where's that breeze coming from?" she asked, as an icy wind blew through the arena.

"There's frost on the ground!" Kirsty exclaimed, pointing to the white sparkly crystals at their feet.

Everyone stared up at the sky as a figure approached, speeding through the air.

"It's Jack Frost!" Rachel realized.

Beginnings and Endings

Jack Frost landed in the arena and stomped his feet. "If it hadn't been for you interfering, I'd have won the Olympics this year," he snarled at Kirsty and Rachel. "The golden cup of luck would have been mine!"

The queen gave him a stern look. "Your team will have to play by the

rules like every other team in the
games," she told him.

Jack Frost ignored her and stomped
toward the girls with his wand raised.
"I'm fed up with you two messing up
my plans!" he shouted. He pointed his
wand at them. "So now I'm going to—"

"You're not going to do anything!"
the queen interrupted, waving her
own wand. The crowd gasped as
Jack Frost's wand flew straight into
the queen's hand.

"I'll look after this while the games are taking place," she told Jack Frost firmly. "I'm not going to let you disrupt the Olympics any further!"

Jack Frost scowled at her, but without his wand he could do nothing but turn and storm off to the spectators' area.

"He knows when he's beaten," Gemma said in a low voice.

"And now the games can begin!" the king declared.

Gemma winked at the girls. "That's my cue," she said, and shot up into the air. She was joined by the other six Sports Fairies — Helena, Stacey, Zoe, Brittany, Samantha, and Alice — and they all twirled up toward the clouds.

Rachel and Kirsty watched as the fairies then flew back down to the arena in an amazing rainbow of colors. They sprinkled fairy dust over the athletes lining up for the opening parade, then wrote GOOD LUCK in large glittery letters in the sky.

"Please stand for the singing of the Fairyland Olympic Anthem," Queen Titania said, and the audience rose to their feet.

A goblin walked to the center of the stage, with a microphone in his hand. He cleared his throat and began to sing.

Rachel elbowed Kirsty and grinned. "It's the goblin we met when we helped Rebecca the Rock 'n' Roll Fairy," she whispered. "Remember?"

Kirsty nodded. "Yes, the one who loved to sing Elvis songs!" she said with a grin.

The goblin took a deep bow as he finished singing, and the crowd cheered—Rachel and Kirsty loudest of all.

Then the queen presented the girls with a glittering silver wand. "Girls, we would be honored if you would light the Olympic flame for us," she said. "And there are some fairies who would love to help you . . ."

As she finished speaking, Rachel and Kirsty both gasped. Flying into the arena was Ruby the Red Fairy, the first fairy they'd ever met, with her Rainbow sisters. Behind them came all the Weather Fairies, and then Katie the Kitten Fairy flew in, waving at the girls as she was joined by the other Pet Fairies. More and more of the girls'

fairy friends flew into the arena!

Kirsty couldn't stop smiling as she greeted them all. "I think every fairy we've ever helped is here with us," she said happily to Rachel.

Rachel had a lump in her throat. "It's so nice to see you again!" she said, throwing her arms around Lucy the Diamond Fairy.

Once all the fairies had arrived, the queen directed them to touch their wands together, along with the silver wand that Rachel and Kirsty were holding.

Rachel held her breath. As all the wands came together, a spark appeared at the end of the special silver wand.

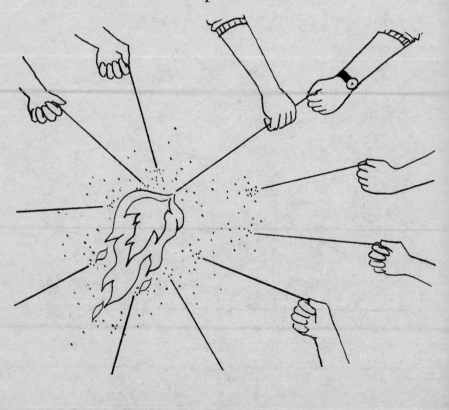

Then the other fairies moved aside,
and the girls took the lit wand to a
sparkling silver cauldron. They
touched the wand to the
cauldron. In a flash of
rainbow-colored
sparkles, a roaring
flame flared up. It
then settled down
to burn steadily.

There was a round
of applause from the crowd, and the
fairies flew up into the air again,
calling out their good-byes.

King Oberon and Queen Titania
came over to the girls. "It's time for you
to go home now," the king said, "but
you'll find one last surprise waiting for
you there."

"Thank you," Kirsty said, curtsying. "We've really enjoyed helping the Sports Fairies," added Rachel. "We're all very grateful to you," the queen said. "Good-bye, girls!" "Good-bye!" Rachel and Kirsty replied.

Then the king waved his wand, and the girls were swept up in a whirlwind and carried gently home.

They found themselves outside Rachel's school, in their normal clothes, each holding a sparkly gold envelope.

Kirsty opened hers eagerly, as did Rachel. Inside they found glittering silver tickets. "*All-access pass to the Fairyland Olympics*," Kirsty read aloud.

"Wow!" Rachel said, beaming. "We can go to any event we choose."

"Oh!" Kirsty gasped. "What a great surprise!"

A light gust of wind made the tickets flutter in their fingers, and they heard Gemma's silvery voice on the breeze. "All you have to do is hold your ticket and wish, and you'll be back at the Fairyland Arena," she whispered.

Kirsty and Rachel smiled in delight. "I'm so happy we'll get to see the events," Rachel said, as they started to walk home.

"Me, too," Kirsty agreed. She grinned at her best friend. "I especially want to see how the goblin gymnastics team performs. After all, they did have some excellent coaching!"

RAINBOW
magic™

THE PARTY FAIRIES

Rachel and Kirsty helped all seven
Sports Fairies . . . but now the Party
Fairies are in trouble! Can Rachel
and Kirsty help

Cherry

the Cake Fairy?

Join their next adventure in this
special sneak peek!

A Birthday Surprise

"I just know this is going to be a wonderful birthday!" Kirsty Tate exclaimed happily, her eyes shining.

Mrs. Tate laughed across the breakfast table. "You've only been awake for half an hour, Kirsty," she said.

"I know," Kirsty replied. "But look at all these cards I've gotten already! Plus there's my party this afternoon. And best of all, Rachel's here for a whole week!" She grinned at her best friend, Rachel Walker, who was sitting next to her.

The girls finished their breakfast and went to get dressed. Rachel was halfway up the stairs behind Kirsty, when she noticed another envelope coming through the mail slot. She ran to get it. It was a beautiful, sparkly gold envelope, and it felt heavy in her hand. She glanced curiously at the front—and then gasped in surprise. *Miss Kirsty Tate and Miss Rachel Walker*, read the beautiful loopy handwriting. Rachel blinked. A card for Kirsty *and* for her? But it wouldn't be her birthday for another three months!

Rachel raced up the stairs two at a

time, thinking about the card. She didn't recognize the handwriting, so it couldn't be from her mom or dad. But who else knew that she was staying with Kirsty?

"Look," cried Rachel, bursting into Kirsty's bedroom. "Another card—and it's for both of us!"

Rachel's fingers trembled with excitement as she carefully broke the wax seal. As soon as the envelope was open, glittering clouds of fairy dust floated into the air, followed by a rainbow that soared across the room.

RAINBOW magic™

SPECIAL EDITION

Three Books in One—
More Rainbow Magic Fun!

Joy the Summer Vacation Fairy — by Daisy Meadows

Holly the Christmas Fairy — by Daisy Meadows

Kylie the Carnival Fairy — by Daisy Meadows

Stella the Star Fairy — by Daisy Meadows

Shannon the Ocean Fairy — by Daisy Meadows

Trixie the Halloween Fairy — by Daisy Meadows

Gabriella the Snow Kingdom Fairy — by Daisy Meadows

Juliet the Valentine Fairy — by Daisy Meadows

Mia the Bridesmaid Fairy — by Daisy Meadows

Flora the Dress-Up Fairy — by Daisy Meadows

■SCHOLASTIC

www.scholastic.com

www.rainbowmagiconline.com

HiT entertainment

RMSPECIAL3

These activities are magical!
Play dress-up, send friendship notes, and much more!

SPECIAL EDITION

Three Books in One!
More Rainbow Magic Fun!

■SCHOLASTIC
www.scholastic.com
www.rainbowmagiconline.com

HIT entertainment

RMSPECIAL2